For Má and Jen—all my stories began with you.

—L.T.

For the newest members of my family:
Sofyan, Esther, and John.

—C.N.

TABLE OF CONTENTS

CHAPTER 1
Go Kings Go!

BUZZZZZZZZZZ

Yes! It's my shift!

The feeling of my blades on the ice is the best as I skate toward the centre line. My teammate Kayden beats me there, so he takes the faceoff to start the third period. I line up on his left like a tiger, ready to pounce. Go Kings Go!

Puck drop!

The Eagles player shoots the puck over our blue line. My teammate Emma stops it and passes it up to Kayden. He bolts to the Eagles' end. I go with Kayden.

An Eagles guy bumps Kayden from the side. He takes the puck back to our end. I'm like a dragon as I change direction and chase after him. My friend Nam and Emma are all over the Eagles players. Everyone is bunching up around our net.

Dad's voice is in my head—*Stay open, buddy!*

I glide to the right side. The Eagles' number 7 has the puck. He trips over his stick and crashes into Nam. The puck is loose. It's coming right at me!

This is it! My chance!

I rake the puck to me. Turn around. Skate to the Eagles' end. Everyone is crowded around our net still. I take the puck up the side.

It's just me. My heart is racing. I'm so fast. I'm a horse in the Vietnamese zodiac dashing across the ice.

I'm close to the net. Stop quick. Look at the far corner. Aim. And shoot!

The goalie dives toward me. The puck slides across the line.

I score!

I raise both hands in the air. My heart is bursting with joy, and everyone is cheering and clapping. It's my first goal of the season!

"Way to go, Jacob!" Kayden says behind me. I high-five him and Emma and Nam too.

My shift ends, and I skate back to the bench and look over at the bleachers. Grandpa Nội claps. He holds up four fingers on each hand. I know he means my jersey number. "Number 8 lucky!" Grandpa Nội said when I first got it last month in October. Usually, only Dad comes to my games. I love when Grandpa Nội comes too.

After the game, I feel okay that we lost. I scored!

"You saw it? My goal?" I ask Dad as he helps me take off my hockey stuff in the dressing room.

"Great job, buddy. Up the side! Like I said!" He smiles.

Dad keeps saying he wanted to play hockey when he was a kid, but he was too poor. So he's really excited. He used to like hockey more than I did, but now I like hockey a lot.

Nam and his dad are beside us. "Good goal, Jacob!" Nam's dad, Chú Văn adds.

"Cám ơn, Chú." I say thank you, one of the only things I can say in Vietnamese.

As Dad takes off my helmet, my hair gets stuck.

"Ouch, Dad!" I rub my head.

Dad starts to take off my neck guard and shoulder pads. "Your hair. We have to cut it or tie it."

"I don't want to cut it. It's the helmet." I swing my legs, pretending I'm a monkey playing around. "It's too small."

"I guess you'll need a new one. We'll go this weekend." He takes off my skates.

"I know what kind I want." I look over at Emma as her mom puts her awesome helmet in her hockey bag.

New helmet! New team! This hockey year is going to be great!

CHAPTER 2
Getting My Way

"Jacob? Ready to get your helmet?" Dad asks me Sunday afternoon as he and Mom clean up our lunch of rice noodles with grilled pork and fish sauce.

"Almost, Dad," Anne says before I can talk.

I'm in the dining room, cleaning Grandma Nội's altar. I take the washcloth and wipe her picture frame and the incense holder, my bottom

lip between my teeth as I focus. I don't like people speaking for me. I frown and spill some of the ashes on the altar table.

Anne, my oldest sister, watches me closely like a cat. She's so picky. Now that I'm eight and in grade three, Anne says this is my job. My other sister, Liz, who is nine and in grade four now, used to have this job. Liz says Anne thinks she's the boss of us.

I want to ask Anne, who is eleven and in grade six, what her job is, but I know that's not how it works in our family.

I wipe up the ashes. Dad and Mom say we Vietnamese believe the spirits of our family, our ancestors, stay with us after they pass away. Grandma Nội died over two years ago but she stares at me every day from her altar picture. She's fuzzy in my memory, more of a feeling than a person.

"Can you pick up Liz from Rohan's on the way home?" Mom asks Dad from the kitchen.

Dad puts on his boots at the front door. "Sure, if we ever get to the store! Come on, buddy!"

"He's done now," Anne says.

Grrrr. I think of a buffalo, silent and staring. That's not me. I can talk for myself.

At the sports store, I sit on the bench as Dad looks at different sizes and styles of helmets. I'm swinging my legs again like a monkey. When I get home, I want to draw monkeys swinging around trees.

"Black again? Or white this time?" He holds up two different helmets.

"I want that one. Like Emma has." I point to a helmet on the shelf behind Dad. It's so nice. With this helmet on, I could be like a bright dragon flying across the ice. No one could catch me. It'd be awesome!

"The pink one!" I add.

Dad doesn't say anything.

"That one. THE PINK ONE," I say again, louder this time.

"Jacob?" Dad whispers.

"That's a girl's helmet!" an older boy sitting at the next bench says out loud.

"Alex!" A grown-up, probably his dad, says to him. "Enough."

"But it is," Alex keeps going.

His dad pulls him up and they walk away.

"I like pink," I say, crossing my arms across my chest. I wear Anne's old shirts all the time. Some of them are pink.

Dad is not saying yes. Dad *always* says yes to me.

"I don't know. You'll have this helmet for a while," he says finally. He looks around and then shifts from one leg to the other, like a dog ready to run.

My heart is beating fast. I stand up. "I don't want black or white." I stomp my left foot. "I want the pink helmet."

Dad checks his phone. "We have to pick up Liz. Let's think about it and come back later."

Dad throws on my toque and rushes me out of the store.

Why am I not getting my way?

CHAPTER 3

Grandma Nội's Gift

When we get home, Anne is painting her nails in the family room. I'm still mad I didn't get what I wanted. Liz tried to tell jokes in the car, but I just looked out the window and kicked my legs.

"Can I do mine too?" Liz asks and sits across from Anne at the low table.

"Be careful!" Anne says. She has pink nails, like the color of bubble gum.

Liz is picking out like seven different colors.

"Can I have blue and pink, all glitter?" I say and sit down next to Anne. I like painting too, so my monkey drawings can wait.

Dad looks at me. "You have school tomorrow. Will you wipe it off before then?"

"Why does he have to?" Liz asks. "Mom lets me wear nail polish to school."

"Boys don't wear nail polish. I haven't seen any with it on," Anne says softly.

"But they can," Liz replies.

Anne pauses and then nods.

"I've painted my nails before," I say back.

"When you were younger," says Dad as he looks around. "Where's Mom? Let's ask her."

I stand up. "First the helmet. Now this! Not

fair!" I stomp all the way upstairs. Mom hears me and comes out of her room.

"Jacob, baby, what's wrong?" She tries to hug me.

"I'm not a baby!" I yell. I slam the door to my room.

I look around at my stuffies, hockey posters, drawings on the wall, and pencils and paper everywhere.

I breathe in and out. I don't get it. It's just a stupid color. But I want it. I *always* get what I want!

My heart feels like when I spill my hot chocolate before I can drink it. Grrrrrr!

I flop down on my bed, my face in my pillow. Something hits me on the back of my head.

Oww.

It's the painted fan, Grandma Nội's gift to me. Somehow it got knocked off the shelf above my bed. I wonder . . .

I pick it up. It has a wooden frame, and it's very old. I open it and it's blue like the sky.

The twelve animals of the Vietnamese zodiac are painted in black ink across the fan. I used to play with it like all the time, pretending to be each animal. Not so much now. Rat, Buffalo, Tiger, Cat,

Dragon, Snake, Horse, Goat, Monkey, Rooster, Dog, and Pig.

There is an animal for each year, in a twelve-year cycle, over and over again. Each animal has a different personality. I don't really know those. I just think about what the animals are like in real life. And I was born in the year of the horse.

Grandma Nội is also a horse, born a long time before me. Dad tells me that's one of the ways Grandma and I are alike. Maybe that's why I got the fan. Anne got her jade bangle and Liz got her pearl earrings.

Dad tells me to talk to Grandma when we light incense, but I never know what to say. Not like Anne, who seems to listen every once in a while, and whisper to Grandma, like when I help her cook one of Grandma Nội's recipes.

Mostly, I remember Grandma Nội when I play with my fan. I remember her warm hugs and hair curling along her neck. My heart feels better thinking about it, warm like when I drink hot chocolate after tobogganing.

I look at the animals on the fan. I wonder . . .

I start at one end of the fan and trace the figure of the rat with my finger. My whole body shivers. Something amazing happens. I can't believe my eyes!

CHAPTER 4
Something Mysterious

The rat turns a glittering gold color. It almost leaps into the air. Then it turns black again.

Wow. Cool!

I feel air blowing on my hair, like rushing wind. I look out the window. It's snowing outside but it's not windy. And my window is shut. As Liz would say, that's sooo weird! I throw the fan on my desk, creeped out a bit.

Then I feel something like an invisible blanket warm out of the dryer wrapped over my shoulders. It feels really nice. Familiar. Like I'm not alone.

Wait a second . . . Grandma Nội! That's what this feeling is! She used to stand behind me when I sat down to draw. She would put her hands on my shoulders and hug me from behind.

I start to pace, walking from one side of the room to the other. That probably isn't supposed to happen, right? Feeling a hug from my dead grandmother?

I run my hands through my hair. My hands are sweaty.

I breathe in and out. I wonder . . . Can I make that feeling happen again? What's the worst that could happen?

I pick up the fan again.

I remember dancing with it after my older cousin Hanh showed me videos of her old fan dances. It's fun dancing, like how I feel gliding on hockey skates.

I start at the beginning, and I trace the rat again. It glitters gold then turns black. Next, I try the buffalo beside it. Then the tiger. They all glitter.

The wind rushes again. What's going on?

I remember when Grandma Nội first showed me the fan. She told me her dad painted the animals on it. She held my hand with her hand, and we would trace the animals together.

Every time I got mad at myself for a drawing that wasn't good, she told me her dad got better and I would too. Now I love drawing. It helps my mind quiet down when it's like a storm, like a blizzard, inside my head.

Something mysterious has changed, I can feel it. Like a door being opened or like birthday candles being lit.

I trace the cat next, almost feeling Grandma's hand on mine.

I trace the dragon and then the snake beside it, watching them glitter gold.

I trace the horse. Instead of just glittering gold, it seems like the horse gallops off the page and runs in circles around me, leaving a trail of glitter. Amazing!

The strange feeling of Grandma Nội here but not here, hugging me from behind, happens again.

The horse makes me feel like I can do anything. I imagine feeling like that, so happy inside, when I wear the pink helmet. I smile.

"Is that you, Grandma? Are you sending me a clue about the helmet?" I whisper out loud. Grandma Nội and I are both horses. "You know that I really want it?"

CHAPTER 5
What Else Can the Fan Do?

Mom said she named all of us after characters from her favorite story books. Anne is from *Anne of Green Gables* and Liz is Elizabeth from *The Paper Bag Princess*. My name comes from *Jacob Two-Two Meets the Hooded Fang*. I don't like how in that story Jacob has to say everything twice just to be heard. People talk over me too. But unlike Jacob Two-Two, I usually get whatever I want. So I'm sure I'll have my helmet soon.

Before dinner the next day, I'm playing with the fan in the family room when Dad comes in.

"Buddy, can you come talk to us?" Dad waves me into his office. Mom is already waiting there.

Oh no, it's going to be serious. Whenever they call my sisters into the office, there's a lot of feelings that happen there. Usually crying or yelling or both. Mom usually leaves the room with her eyes red and holding tissues.

Liz and Anne are putting out bowls and chopsticks, rice, meat, veggies for dinner. And they give me a look like, "You got this!"

"Sit down, buddy." Dad points to his couch.

Mom starts. "Let's talk about what happened when you went to get your helmet."

"Please, Dad, I really want the pink one," I say.

"Why, baby?" Mom asks.

I shrug. "I just like it. It's bright and fun!"

"At the store, I was . . . surprised," Dad says.

"Okay," I say.

"We're okay that you want a helmet that's pink," Mom says, sitting down beside me.

I think of the fan and how I can be like the horse I am. "I'll feel so happy when I wear it."

They look at each other, like there's more to say.

"We don't want you to be sad that other people may be surprised," Mom adds.

"Why? Because they think it's a girl color. That's dumb. It's just a color."

"It is dumb." Dad nods. "But people may still say things to you."

"I don't care," I reply. I think I'll look like a pink pig, no, like a cool hockey-playing pig!

Dad looks at Mom, who nods. "Okay, buddy, let's go get your pink helmet! We'll be quick!"

"Yes!" I jump around the room. I *do* get what I want!

"Remember, you can tell us anything." Mom hugs me.

Mom and Dad say that all the time now. Something happened when Anne changed ballet schools a couple years ago. We hug a lot more too.

The fan helped me out! What else can the fan do?

After dinner, I wear my new helmet around the house.

Liz is practicing Taekwondo in the basement. She's a yellow belt now. Anne is sitting on the couch playing the same old role-playing game she always does on her laptop.

"So, you okay?" Anne asks me.

"Did you get into trouble? I didn't hear crying!" Liz adds.

"I'm great. I got what I wanted," I say, pointing to my helmet.

"Nice!" Anne says.

I decide to tell my sisters my secret. "You know the fan Grandma Nội left me?"

"It's not as cool as my pearl earrings, but yes," Liz says.

I sigh.

"Or as nice as my jade bangle," Anne adds, laughing.

I ignore her. "I think the fan has a mysterious power."

They both stop what they're doing and turn to look at each other.

"Oh really?" Liz says to me.

I nod a few times. "It's sending me clues, to help me get what I want."

Liz smiles. She's only a year older than me but she thinks she knows *so* much more than me.

"What?" I ask.

"And is it windy at all when you hold the fan?" Anne asks.

How does she know?

"Yes, for sure! Why?" I ask.

"Anne told me last year. That's Grandma Nội. The painted fan connects you to her. Like my earrings and Anne's bangle," Liz replies.

"This happens to you too? You never told me," I say.

"It's different for each of us. So we were waiting

to see how it was for you." Anne shrugs like it's no big deal.

"If you need help, Grandma Nội will know," Liz says.

CHAPTER 6
Why Can't I Do What I Want?

On Saturday, I'm so excited for my hockey game, like a goat waiting to escape its pen. I know Mom and Dad said some people may not like my helmet, but I don't care. I LIKE it.

In the dressing room, Dad helps me put on my gear. I take the helmet out of my bag.

"Emma, look!" I say and hold up my helmet.

"Cool!" She gives me a thumbs-up. "We're helmet twinsies!"

"Why did you get that?" Nam asks as he sits beside me. His dad looks at my dad and says something in rapid Vietnamese. I can't follow. My dad says something back quickly.

"That's for girls!" Kayden calls from across the room. He begins to laugh.

"Jacob's a girl!" Olivia points at me and starts to laugh. Her giggles are high pitched and hurt my ears.

"Hey, we don't say stuff like that," Coach Mike says to everyone in the room.

My teammates are quiet. But some still give me funny looks, like they're not sure about me anymore.

My cheeks are flushed. I feel hot now with all this equipment on.

"You okay, buddy?" Dad asks me.

I nod but don't say anything.

In the middle of the game, someone shouts out, "Way to go, girls!" when I pass the puck to Emma and she scores.

After that, I catch an edge on my skate and fall hard. Then I miss the puck as Emma passes to me. This is not a good time. I can't focus, still thinking about the kids laughing at me. I don't feel like the bright dragon I thought I would. I want to go hide instead.

After the game, in the dressing room, no one looks at me.

Dad finishes taking off my skates. His phone

rings. "Wait there, buddy. I have to take this," he says and goes into the hallway. Grandpa Nội is waiting for us there.

Nam and his dad and me are the only ones left in the room. They moved here from Vietnam a few years ago. I've never been to Vietnam. Nam teaches me Vietnamese words. I teach him things I know about, like hockey and pizza.

Nam's dad, Chú Văn looks at me. "Jacob, Vietnamese boy strong. No wear pink. Okay?" He takes Nam by the arm and they leave before I can say anything. Before Dad comes back.

I feel sadness like a weight on my chest. I didn't think I would care what people said. But I do.

On Sunday, I'm watching the Winnipeg Jets game with Grandpa Nội. He's put together my favorite snacks—seaweed, rice crackers, cheddar cheese, bites of Chinese sausage, and sour gummies.

"School good?" he asks as we sit close together.

I nod.

"Hockey good?"

I shrug.

He looks at me. "Why hockey no good?"

I shrug again. I think about all the kids laughing and Chú Văn's words.

"Tell me," he says, and holds my hand.

"People laugh at my pink helmet. Mom wants to cut my hair. I can't wear nail polish. Why are things girl things or boy things?" I don't know if he understands all the English words. I wish I had more Vietnamese words. "Why can't I do what I want anymore, Grandpa?" I begin to cry. I didn't think I would.

He nods his head. He wipes away my tears and hugs me. "Jacob okay. Ông Nội loves Jacob."

CHAPTER 7
Am I Weird?

"Hey, Jacob, shouldn't your boots and hat be pink too?" Kayden yells as he runs toward me across the field during afternoon recess on Thursday.

"Since you like it so much!" Olivia adds.

They have both been bugging me all week. I wish Emma went to this school too.

Nam and I are making a pile of leaves, but he walks away when they start talking.

"Leave him alone!" Liz says, coming over.

Rohan adds, "Can't you just stop? It's not a big deal."

Anne and my cousin Hao start to walk over too after noticing us all together. Kayden and Olivia run off.

I pull my hoodie up and wish I could turn into a snake and slither away.

At the recess bell, we go back to Mrs. Goodman's class. Liz had her as a teacher last year. Mrs. Goodman said at the beginning of the school year she was happy with "another Nguyen kid." But I don't like being in my sister's shadow.

I also don't like when people think they know me. Like everyone thinks me and Nam should be friends because we're the only Vietnamese kids

in the class and are always put together. I don't know if we would be friends on our own. Nam doesn't look at me as we walk in. Maybe he's not my friend.

After school, Mom drives all of us over to Auntie Hai's house. Grandpa Nội lives with her, but too bad he's napping when we get there. Mom leaves with Hao and Anne somewhere, and Auntie Hai takes Liz to the nail salon. I'm home with my cousin Hanh.

In the kitchen, I look in the pantry and take out a package of seaweed and some shrimp crackers. I'm like a rat, always looking for more food.

"Hey, bé Jacob!" Hanh says as she comes into the kitchen.

She always calls me that. It means baby in Vietnamese, and I don't like it.

"Hello, Chị Hanh!" I say. She makes me use the Vietnamese word for older sister/older cousin that I don't use with Anne or Liz. Their family is more into Vietnamese stuff than our family is.

"Wanna help me with this poster?" She unrolls a large piece of white poster board and puts down a bunch of markers. "I know I could use the printers at school, but handmade stuff is cool too."

"Sure." I stuff crackers in my mouth really fast. Hanh is in grade twelve and is so cool. I want purple streaks in my hair like she has.

She starts outlining bubble letters.

"What is GSA?" I ask and start filling in the G with polka dots.

"It's a club at school," she responds. She starts writing in a time and date at the bottom of the poster. "Can you add some hearts and rainbows too?" she asks.

"Sure. What's the club about?" I ask. She knows a lot of things I don't know anything about.

She stops to think and tilts her head to one side like Auntie Hai does. "For you, bé, it's where

students of all different genders can meet and talk in a safe space. And we can work together to change things that are still unfair."

"Genders? Like boy and girl?" I ask.

"Not just boy or girl. Could be others. Like nonbinary or gender fluid. People think of themselves all different ways," she replies.

I don't understand everything she says. "More than boy or girl? More than just two? I didn't know that."

She nods. "That's okay. We're learning all the time about people and learning about ourselves. It's not easy."

I feel my heart beating fast. I wonder. "So if I like pink, what does that mean?" I whisper. "Am I weird?"

"Oh, bé! You're amazing! You can like what you like and dress how you want. It's all okay." She puts her hand over mine. "We can all express ourselves however we want. Be who we are."

But who am I? Like the animals of the zodiac on my fan, there are so many different ways to be!

"Now keep coloring!" Hanh says, and we both burst out laughing.

CHAPTER 8
The Fan Dance

On Sunday, we're having dinner at home. Like we're celebrating Christmas. Anne and Dad have been cooking a lot with Mom and Auntie Hai.

Hanh is on her phone. Uncle Hai, Liz, and Hao are in the basement playing video games.

I just stay out of the way. No one expects me to help. I'm sitting with Grandpa Nội.

"Zodiac animals," I say, pointing to my drawings of the animals from my painted fan.

"Horse you. Happy," Grandpa Nội says, pointing at the drawing of the horse then pointing at me. "Me Goat. Smart. Your dad Monkey. Funny."

I laugh and he smiles.

"Dinner time," Anne says. She puts some of the food on Grandma Nội's altar and lights the incense. There's bánh xèo fold-over thin pancakes, chả giò spring rolls, salad, barbecue duck, bread, fried rice, and đồ chua pickled veggies.

"The bánh xèo is your best yet, Anne," Mom says as we sit around the table.

"Very tasty," Uncle Hai adds.

"Ngon quá," Grandpa Nội agrees.

"I made the salad!" Liz says in a loud voice. She always thinks Mom pays more attention to Anne.

"Love the salad. More please," Auntie Hai says.

And Auntie Hai is always nice to Liz.

Liz smiles.

"Sooooo . . ." Hanh starts. "I still have spots to fill in the fan dance for Tết. Anne? Liz? Will you do it? Please? I need bodies."

"At the Buddhist temple?" Dad asks.

Auntie Hai nods. "Hanh no dance this year. She teach younger girls."

I know Auntie Hai's family goes to temple all the time. We don't.

"Lunar New Year is late January this year,"

Mom says, looking at the calendar. "Is that enough time to learn the dance?"

Hanh nods. "It's just for fun. Not like Anne's ballet. So?"

"Sure," Anne says.

"No way!" Liz says at the same time.

The whole table laughs.

I don't laugh. How come Hanh doesn't ask me or Hao? She only asked the girls. She's done the fan dance with me at home. I'm sad, like a cat in the rain. I love the fan dance. I feel good when I'm dancing.

Isn't that what she talks about at her GSA club? People can be who they are.

"Okay, Jacob?" Grandpa Nội asks me.

I shake my head. "I think I ate too much. I'll be in my room." I leave the table.

When I shut the door, I hold my painted fan. I breathe in and out.

I wonder . . . will Grandma Nội help me?

I trace all the animals with my finger, starting with the rat at one end. It glitters gold for a bit. I feel a warm presence around me, hugging me. The wind rushes by me.

I trace all the animals to get to the horse. This time, the horse only glitters gold. I feel like I need to keep going, tracing the goat and the monkey next. They glitter. Next I trace the rooster. It almost leaps into the air, flapping around me. It throws back its head and crows and crows.

Roosters can be really loud. I remember reading that in my book about farm animals. Roosters wake up people at sunrise.

The rooster uses its voice and people listen!

That's it! "Thank you, Grandma Nội!" I say out loud.

I leave my room, holding the painted fan in my hands, and stand in front of the TV, which everyone is sitting around.

I breathe in and out. "I want to be in the fan dance," I say to the whole family.

CHAPTER 9

What's Wrong with Me?

"Great goal, Emma!" I say. We're changing out of our gear after winning a game. I didn't get any goals, but I got one assist.

"Thanks," she replies.

"Go Kings Go!" Kayden shouts from the other side of the room.

I look at Emma and Olivia, the only girls on the team. I wonder how they feel being a King.

Maybe they want to be a Queen instead? Thinking about Hanh and her GSA club, why don't we have a team name that includes everyone?

I take off my own skates since Dad is outside the dressing room on a call, again.

I think my favorite part of skating is the feeling of gliding on the ice, like a snake in water, fast and smooth. I can't wait to dance. I think I'll feel the same way—free.

Mom and Dad said they have to think about letting me do the fan dance. Like with the pink helmet. But I'm sure I'll get what I want.

Nam and his dad are about to leave. I wave quickly but keep my head down. I still remember Chú Văn doesn't like my pink helmet.

"Nam, wait in the car?" Chú Văn says. We're

the only ones in the dressing room.

"Nam say you do fan dance. No, Jacob, don't do. You boy, you not girl. Girls do fan dance. Do Taekwondo like sister. Vietnamese boys strong. If they see you weak, will laugh. You will hurt. Don't want you to hurt." His voice is gentle but firm.

I breathe in and out. Like the rooster, I can use my voice. "Chú Văn, why can't I be strong and do the fan dance too?"

Before he can say anything, Dad comes around the corner. "Văn, that's enough!"

Dad and Chú Văn speak in Vietnamese. Dad's been learning and practicing, but he still uses English words sometimes.

Chú Văn walks away.

"I'm sorry, buddy," Dad says.

"Is it really so bad that I want to do the fan dance?" I whisper, peeking up at him.

"No, it's not bad. He shouldn't have said those things to you." He pauses. "Let's not go home yet."

We drive to Assiniboine Park.

"Why are we at the zoo?" I ask as we enter the gates. "It's cold."

"Let's just check on the polar bears." Dad holds my hand as we start walking.

"Okay."

"I'm sorry Chú Văn said those things to you," Dad says as we take off our jackets and stop in front of the bear area. "Let me tell you a story about him."

"Okay." I look down at my boots.

"Chú Văn told me once that when he and Cô Kim and Nam first came to Canada, lots of people were nice to them and welcomed them. But there were some people who were not nice to them. He was standing right here watching the bears when people made fun of him and laughed at him for how he looked and how he dressed. He was carrying a bag that people thought was like a purse. He was scared."

"Grown-ups bully other grown-ups?" I ask.

Dad nods. "Some people think Asian men are weak. He doesn't want people to say that about you. So you don't get hurt like he did. But he still shouldn't have said anything to you. I'm proud of you for speaking up."

"Why do I want to do the fan dance?" I whisper to myself. "What's wrong with me?" I ask.

"Nothing is wrong with you, nothing at all!" He wraps one arm around my shoulders. "If you want to do the fan dance, Mom and I want you to do it," Dad says.

I hug Dad as I think of Grandma Nội's gift showing me the rooster. The fan is still a mystery but one thing I know is that I feel it's helping me. My chest doesn't feel as tight now.

CHAPTER 10

I'm Not a Baby Anymore

Liz squeezes my hand as we walk into the basement of the Buddhist temple on Saturday. It's our first fan dance practice and my heart is racing. I'm glad Liz decided to join too. It's annoying when my sisters speak for me, but I also feel good knowing they're here for me. Other than me, Liz, and Anne, there are five other dancers, all girls.

"Welcome!" Hanh says as she opens a

cardboard box in the middle of the floor. "These are your fans!"

They are red and fluttery. Even though they're different from Grandma Nội's painted fan, they are so beautiful. Hanh does a dance move, waving both fans over her head, and I smile.

Two girls facing me start to giggle.

Another girl, an older one, points at me. "A boy!"

Liz steps in front of me. "Does anyone have a problem with my brother being here?" I see her hands are now fists at her sides.

"Liz, it's okay," Anne adds and then looks at the girls. "We're all here to have fun."

"Hey!" Hanh says gently. "This dance is for anyone who wants to join. Show kindness, please.

We're a team now."

As we start to practice, I feel less and less nervous in my heart. I just feel . . . happy. I feel like when I draw, when the blizzard in my head stops, and my mind is clear. I feel more ME.

After dinner, I'm practicing the fan dance in the living room. I have Grandma Nội's fan in one hand and a fan I made from construction paper in my other hand. Imagining the zodiac animals, I'm a happy horse then a crowing rooster.

Mom finishes the dishes and then watches me. "How was practice?"

"Good," I say, still dancing. Dad is out with

Anne and Liz somewhere.

"You know, I always wanted to dance. To be a prima ballerina."

"I know, Mom. You've told us." I know that's why she wanted Anne and Liz to do ballet, like Dad wanted me to do hockey.

I do all the moves Hanh taught us today, flipping the fan one way then another. It's different from my hockey moves but still fun.

Mom claps when I'm done. "That was beautiful! My baby!"

"I'm not a baby anymore." I put hands on my hips.

"No, you're not." My mom comes closer and looks at me. Really looks at me. "And I can't wait to see who you become."

CHAPTER 11

Lunar New Year

"Chúc mừng năm mới," Anne says to me at breakfast, wishing me a happy new year. Today is Tết and the Lunar New Year show is this weekend. I'm so excited!

I try my best to say it back to her, but the words jumble in my mouth like I'm a sheep trying to talk. Mom says I can soon join the Vietnamese lessons Dad and Anne and Liz take.

Me and Anne and Liz are wearing our áo dài tunics to school. Auntie Hai brought them back from Vietnam the last time they went there. It's a tunic that's cut on both sides that you wear over pants. Anne wears pink. Liz has a sparkly yellow one.

Mine is blue like the deep ocean with a gold pattern like circles. I love how it feels on my skin, smooth and slippery. It's long, going to my knees. I like how my hair just brushes the high collar. It doesn't feel like this with my T-shirts.

At school, I take off my jacket when we get to our classroom. "Happy Lunar New Year!" I yell.

"What are you wearing, Jacob?" Olivia asks.

Kids laugh and point.

"Is that a dress? Are you wearing a dress?" Kayden adds.

"No, it's not. It's an áo dài!" I reply.

Another kid, Adam, joins in. "Ow eye?! You're not making any sense."

"Jacob's a girl!" Olivia says.

I breathe in and out. I think of the horse and the rooster. I'm happy in these clothes, and it's okay to use my voice to say so.

"It's Vietnamese. I'm celebrating." My voice is calm but I'm still a bit shaky inside.

When Mrs. Goodman comes in, everyone stops talking.

"Good morning, class. Today we're going to learn about Lunar New Year."

"Did people say anything about your áo dài?" Mom says as she drives us home.

"Everyone liked it," Liz says.

"Same here," Anne adds.

"What about you, Jacob?" Mom asks.

I shrug but don't say anything. When we get home, I run upstairs to my room and the tears leak out. I like wearing this. It's part of my Vietnameseness. But it's still really hard having people laugh at me. It's like I'm wrong.

No one laughs at Anne and Liz in their áo dài. They get to be beautiful and soft. Why laugh at me? Why am I expected to play in dirt and wear boring stuff and not be weak?

Maybe Chú Văn is right. I don't want to be hurt.

I grab Grandma Nội's painted fan, hoping to get help. My tears fall on the old fabric.

"I just want to be normal, so people don't make fun of me," I say out loud.

CHAPTER 12

I Get It Now

I start at one end of the fan and trace the rat. I expect it will glitter gold as always. Instead, it scurries off into the air, looking for food, not giving up. Wow! I trace the buffalo next, and instead of glittering gold, it shows up in the air, strong and waiting. This is so exciting! I trace the tiger next. It roars!

I feel the rushing wind and Grandma Nội's hands on my shoulders.

I trace all the zodiac animals and it's like all of them float in the air together, like being at the zoo!

"What do these clues mean, Grandma?" I feel the blizzard in my head still. How do I solve this mystery?

I feel Grandma Nội hugging me.

All the animals are different. Using their voices. Being playful. Being strong and patient. Being themselves.

The blizzard in my mind starts to clear up.

I wonder . . . they are all so different. At different times. In different ways.

Wait.

The fan isn't about helping me get what I want. The fan is about showing me that I can be all those things. I can be ME.

That's the mystery of the fan! "I get it now."

The next day at school, I'm sitting by myself at recess, still thinking about what the fan showed me. The wind is very cold.

Nam comes to see me. "Hey."

I look up from jabbing my stick around a pile of snow. "Hey."

"You okay?" he asks.

I nod.

"So, just to tell you . . . I wanted to wear an áo dài yesterday too. I wasn't brave like you," he whispers.

I look up. "You think I'm brave?"

"To do what you want? Yeah!" he says.

"Thanks," I reply.

I smile and he smiles back. He's right. I know what I want and what I can be.

"Costume all ready!" Auntie Hai says after school when we're over at her house. She holds up pale-yellow áo dài tunics with gold thread creating a pattern of clouds at the bottom.

I try mine on and look in the mirror. I love it. My flowing hair. My flowing robes. Like a dragon in the sunshine.

Grandpa comes up behind me. "Jacob." He looks at me in a way I have not seen before. What does he think?

Then he smiles and his eyes are watery. He holds my face in his hands. And I remember Grandma Nội used to do that too.

I feel the rushing wind.

All the ancestors are in you.

Those words are carried on the wind. I feel a warm hand against my heart.

"Jacob. You. Wonderful," Grandpa says and I hug him tight.

CHAPTER 13
Into the Spotlight

It's the night of the Lunar New Year show at the temple. Before the show, we're at Dad's cousin's house and there are so many people—aunties and uncles and cousins and babies. I can't hear it's so loud, and I keep losing Liz and Anne in the crowd.

At Lunar New Year, kids get lucky money and I can't wait to see how much I got. I'm saving up

for a comic book creator set complete with pencils and books to draw in.

I reach for another chả giò spring roll.

"Enough, Jacob. We need to perform," Anne says as I stuff my face.

Anne puts out more food on the table, smiling. I know she's so proud of the chả giò she made.

"Up!" A toddler with pigtails wearing a red áo dài tunic tugs on my pants and raises her arms. I pick her up and she pulls my hair.

I think Liz loves these big parties. She's in the middle of a crowd of cousins showing off her Taekwondo moves. But it's like a herd of buffalo— too much for me!

"Hanh, Liz, Anne, Jacob!" Mom yells and

points to the front door. "Time to get ready for the performance. We have to get to the temple first."

I put the toddler down and she cries.

"See you all there," Mom says to the crowd, and they wave at us as we hurry out.

Waiting outside of the multipurpose room, it's our turn next. It seems like there are dogs chasing each other in my stomach.

The show opened with the múa lân dance. The lân look almost like lions, with big manes and tongues hanging out. There are musicians, and some older girls do the nón lá hat dance.

"You good, Jacob?" Liz whispers beside me.

"No," I answer. I'm suddenly so scared, I can't move. What if everyone laughs? What am I doing here? I should back out.

"You can do this," Liz says.

"You love dancing. The audience will see that," Anne adds.

The rush of wind. It blows around all of us Nguyen kids.

"Grandma Nội," all three of us say at the same time. We giggle, trying to be quiet. We beam and hold each others' hands, creating a circle.

I feel calm again. "I do love it, like I love hockey," I say.

"Okay, ready. Let's go," Cousin Hanh whispers as she signals for the music to begin.

I follow my sisters to the little raised stage, all

of us fluttering our fans. My hands tingle and my heart is beating so fast, like how I feel when I'm on the ice, excited but a bit nervous. I step into the spotlight, the soft fabric moving around me. I take a deep breath in and then let it out slowly. And I begin to dance, going with the music.

I look out at the crowd briefly and see Mom and Dad smiling in the front row. They are proud. Auntie and Uncle Hai, Hao, Grandpa Nội, and other family around the room. They are smiling and clapping.

I think of Grandma Nội's fan and all the animals of the zodiac painted on it. My muscles relax, and I start to grin. I'm a strong horse, then a soft cat, a gliding snake, then a happy monkey. I can be all those things too, at different times, in different ways. I can be powerful and graceful, strong and soft. I can be who I am.

CHAPTER 14

My Ancestors

It's been a few months since Lunar New Year. It's now late April and the snow is gone. I see buds of leaves and flowers all around. Things are changing. And Dad says we're all going to Vietnam for summer vacation.

I'm cleaning the altar for Grandma Nội. Today is her death anniversary and we are putting together a big dinner. Auntie Hai's family is coming over and so are some of Dad's cousins and their families.

I want to tell my family something and today seems like a good time. Everyone is around.

I stand in the middle of the living room. "I have something to say."

My family is busy getting stuff ready. They stop. Anne and Liz put down the dishes they are carrying. Mom and Dad sit on the couch, and they look unsure.

"I don't want to be called Jacob anymore," I say.

No one says anything. Dad starts to speak but I see Mom put her hand on his hands. He remains quiet.

"Why?" Liz finally asks.

I shrug. "I don't like it anymore. It's like my baby name. I just want to be Jay."

"Why?" Liz asks again.

"That's enough, Liz!" Mom warns.

I shrug again. "I just don't think my name fits. I don't know what fits me now."

"And that's okay. We will call you Jay," Dad says.

Mom nods. "And we can keep talking about this, as you figure out what fits," she adds. "And we love you."

"I love you all too," I say. I feel like I can breathe easier now, like a horse breaking free.

Liz traps me in a tiger hug and Anne joins in.

Dad lights five joss sticks and hands one of the skinny incense sticks to me. I see all the other family members close their eyes to say their prayers.

On Grandma Nội's altar, there are three ceramic bowls of jasmine rice, three cups of black tea, bánh xèo, đồ chua, chả giò, and Anne's newest dish, chè đậu trắng rice pudding.

Our ancestors stay with us after they pass away. They hear our prayers. They watch out for us. I close my eyes and even though I'm not tracing the animals on the fan, I feel Grandma Nội around me. I know my ancestors love me.

I see Anne wearing her jade bangle. I see Liz wearing her pearl earrings. My painted fan is folded up and sticking out of the left pocket of my new pants. These are Grandma Nội's gifts to all of us.

My grandma's real gift is her wish for me to be who I really am. I wish for that too.

All About Jacob
and His Family

Jacob Nguyen is eight years old and he's in grade three. One of the best things about playing hockey is going for noodles after the games with Dad and Grandpa Nội. In springtime, he loves to walk outside in the rain and then look for rainbows.

Liz Nguyen is nine years old and she's in grade four. She's working on coding mini sports games like shooting basketballs or scoring soccer goals on the computer. Her fave thing about spring is riding her bike with her friends searching for ducklings and goslings.

Anne Nguyen is eleven years old and she's in grade six. She's learning how to knit and is working on scarves for all her family and friends. She's super excited for spring as she's planting her own garden and can't wait to start cooking with the vegetables she's growing.

Cousin Hanh is seventeen years old and she's in grade twelve. She volunteers at the children's hospital and the Buddhist temple. When spring comes, she'll be busy applying to universities and colleges for next year and is excited for new possibilities.

Cousin Hao is eleven years old and he's in grade six. He's really into reading and collecting comics and gets lost in the imaginary worlds. His favorite activity during spring is playing soccer. It's so fun making quick choices and fast moves as the goalie.

Mom works with computers in a tall building downtown. Her happy place is at the gym, especially the hot yoga studio. Her idea of a fun vacation is being near water and not having to cook all the time.

Dad is a lawyer who helps people from all over the world come to Canada. His favorite foods are any kind of noodles and sauce, yum! He's never had a dog before and has always wanted a black Lab.

Grandma Nội is the best cook and she would sometimes eat dessert first before eating dinner. She collected figurines of the Vietnamese zodiac and áo dài fabric. She used to tell a lot of stories about the family and Vietnamese fairy tales.

Grandpa Nội likes to grow flowers, fruits, and vegetables. He misses the feeling of the open, blue sky like when he lived on a farm in Vietnam. He can't wait for hockey playoffs every year.

Auntie Hai works at a nail salon painting people's nails. Her favorite color is red: a lucky color. She writes poetry in Vietnamese about love and family.

Uncle Hai's job is helping care for people at the hospital. His goal is to take his family back to Vietnam on vacation every three years. He likes taking pictures around the neighborhood and at the Buddhist temple.

Author's Note

Thanks so much for hanging out with Jacob and his family. For his story, I wanted to explore what it means to figure out who you are and what kind of things you like, and to do this when you're surrounded by different expectations and opinions. This is my offering.

Having altars to the ancestors is a Vietnamese custom I grew up with after my dad passed away when I was seven years old. We made offerings of food and recognized death anniversaries. You may have your own special ways to remember loved ones.

As a kid, I loved playing with the set of glass figurines of the twelve Vietnamese zodiac animals in my room. I remember older Vietnamese people would ask me about what animal year I was born in and how interested they were in the answer. Embracing and celebrating this tradition of the zodiac always made me feel connected to Vietnamese culture in a fun and accessible way.

A note about the language in this series: sometimes the Vietnamese words are spelled in Vietnamese with accents, and they are pronounced in Vietnamese. And sometimes the Vietnamese words have no accents and are pronounced in a way that fits with how words are pronounced in English. I've made these choices based on how I imagined the character would say them/think of them.

For example, Nguyen as a last name is written as Nguyễn in Vietnamese. I have chosen to write it as Nguyen without the accents as I imagine the siblings would write it like that at school and pronounce their last name in an English way.

Also, sometimes I have chosen to merge English and Vietnamese words. In Vietnamese, a person would call their dad's mom Bà Nội and their dad's dad Ông Nội. I have merged Grandma and Grandpa with Nội. A person would call their dad's oldest sister Cô Hai and call their dad's oldest sister's husband Dượng Hai. I merged Auntie and Uncle with Hai. I imagine this is a decision Jacob's family made. It may be different with each family.

I'm so honored you chose this book. Feel free to reach out to me at lindaytrinh.com. Take care!

Linda

Acknowledgments

Much gratitude to the entire team at Annick Press for believing in and supporting The Nguyen Kids series and *The Mystery of the Painted Fan*. Thanks to Katie for being such a careful and responsive editor. Thanks to Kaela, Jieun, Eleanor, and Mary Ann for their insights. Thanks to Craig at Rainbow Resource Centre for reading and providing an assessment of the book's exploration of gender and gender expression. Thanks to Clayton for his amazing illustrations.

Love to all my extended family and friends for their support and thanks to those who read various drafts. Deepest appreciation to my writerly friends. Thanks to my best friend Mirna for our long conversations about young readers and for always being there for me. Thanks to my cousins Ky and Bao for their perspectives and encouragement. Thanks to my big sister Jen, my biggest fangirl, for loving all my words and helping me explore our Vietnamese heritage. Thanks to my husband, Ryan, for giving me the space and support to take the chance on myself to be an author.

Thanks to my kids, Lexi and Evan, who inspire me with their curiosity, bravery, kindness, and perseverance. Lexi was my first reader and offered great insights and Evan had great ideas for me. I'm so humbled that they're able to see kids like themselves in this series. Mama loves you! And of course, thanks to my mom, for making this life possible for me, and for showing me every day what hard work looked like when I was growing up.

I'll be forever grateful to my dad, my grandparents, and to all my ancestors, for everything they have sacrificed and accomplished so that I may pursue my dreams!

Look for Book 4 in the series coming in October 2023!

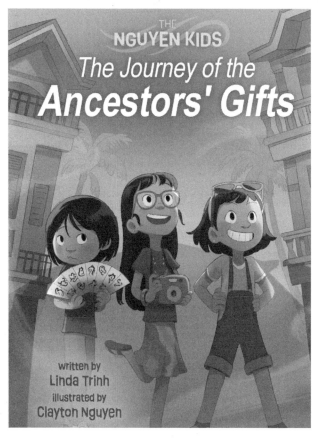

THE NGUYEN KIDS

The Journey of the
Ancestors' Gifts

written by
Linda Trinh
illustrated by
Clayton Nguyen

The Nguyen kids are going on vacation! It's their first time in Vietnam and staying in Grandma Nội's childhood home, and they should be excited—as soon as they enter the house, though, something doesn't feel right. Why can't they connect with Grandma Nội using their gifts, the way they can at home?

About the Author

©Kalla Photography

Linda Trinh is a Vietnamese Canadian author who writes stories for kids and grown-ups. She was born in the Year of the Rooster as part of the Vietnamese zodiac. Her kids were born in the Year of the Cat and the Year of the Horse like two of the Nguyen kids. She enjoyed doing Vietnamese folk dancing when she was younger, and her favorite dance was the fan dance. Dancing helped Linda celebrate her culture. She spends a lot of time staring out her window, daydreaming, and pacing around the house, writing in her head way before she types out anything. She lives with her husband and two kids in Winnipeg.

About the Illustrator

Clayton Nguyen is an artist working on animated TV shows and films to bring imaginary characters and worlds to life. In a complete coincidence, Clayton also started drawing at an early age and has two older sisters, just like Jacob. Being the youngest sibling, he is still sometimes treated like the baby of the family. Some of his earliest memories of becoming interested in art come from watching TV shows like *Art Attack* and anime with his sisters after school. Nowadays, when he isn't drawing, you'll often find him playing video games or getting bubble tea in Toronto.